3 9082 14380 5839

D1613409

Published by Stone Arch Books, an imprint of Capstone
1710 Roe Crest Drive, North Mankato, Minnesota 56003
capstonepub.com

Library of Congress Cataloging-in-Publication Data
Names: Pryor, Shawn, author. | Ficorilli, Francesca, illustrator.
Title: Racing ransom / by Shawn Pryor ; illustrated by Francesca Ficorilli.
Description: North Mankato, Minnesota : Stone Arch Books, an imprint
of Capstone, [2022] | Series: The Gamer | Audience: Ages 8–11. | Audience:
Grades 4–6. | Summary: Cynthia Cyber has trapped two programmers in the
video game Space Racers, which she invented but did not get credit for, and
sends a monster racer to destroy them if she does not get a ten million dollar
ransom—and it is up to thirteen-year-old Tyler Morant in his secret identity
as the Gamer to rescue them before they are destroyed.
Identifiers: LCCN 2021030698 (print) | LCCN 2021030699 (ebook) |
ISBN 9781663977045 (hardcover) | ISBN 9781666329254 (paperback) |
ISBN 9781666329261 (pdf)
Subjects: LCSH: Video games—Juvenile fiction. | Superheroes—Juvenile
fiction. | Supervillains—Juvenile fiction. | Extortion—Juvenile fiction. |
Rescues—Juvenile fiction. | Racing—Juvenile fiction. | CYAC: Video games—
Fiction. | Superheroes—Fiction. | Supervillains—Fiction. | Ransom—Fiction.
| Rescues—Fiction. | Racing—Fiction. | LCGFT: Superhero fiction.
Classification: LCC PZ7.1.P7855 Rac 2022 (print) | LCC PZ7.1.P7855 (ebook)
| DDC 813.6 [Fic]—dc23
LC record available at https://lccn.loc.gov/2021030698
LC ebook record available at https://lccn.loc.gov/2021030699

Designer: Hilary Wacholz

Printed and bound in the USA. PO4608

TABLE OF CONTENTS

You may believe that video games and apps are just harmless fun. But in these special places where we play, a hero works to protect us from the dangers that exist in those worlds . . .

Meet **THE GAMER**, defender of Earth and the digital realm!

REAL NAME: Tyler Morant

HERO NAME: The Gamer

AGE: 13

HERO TOOL: Gamer Activation
Device, which transforms
Tyler into the Gamer

ENEMY: Cynthia Cyber

MISSION: To defeat evil Cynthia Cyber
and her wicked digital monsters

CHAPTER 1

THE KIDNAPPING

In her lair, Cynthia Cyber turns on a power switch.

A **supercomputer** lights up her evil lab.

Cynthia turns toward her tied-up prisoners.

A **giant laser** hums above them.

"Years ago, a young woman named Cynthia Cooper made a game called *Space Racers*," Cynthia tells her prisoners.

The laser **glows**.

"You removed my name from the game and **took the credit**," says Cynthia.

The two prisoners try to speak, but Cynthia quiets them.

"Because of you, Cynthia Cooper became Cynthia Cyber. And now, you will pay!" **screams** Cynthia.

The laser **fires**.

Cynthia's prisoners become part of the *Space Racers* video game.

"Enjoy the game!" Cynthia's laugh fills the room.

CHAPTER 2

ENTER THE SPACE RACE

Elsewhere, Tyler is playing video games at home.

Suddenly his gaming screens **crackle** and **glow**.

"Greetings, gamers! I've taken over the **digital realm** and your favorite game, *Space Racers*," says Cynthia from the screens.

The screens show Cynthia's prisoners, **trapped** inside the game!

Each prisoner is inside a **speedy** space car on the track. They cannot escape.

"My needs are simple," says Cynthia. "The Canvas Software Company must pay me a **ransom** of ten million dollars in the next hour."

"And if they don't, I'll have my monster racer hunt down and **destroy** these worthless programmers I've trapped," she adds.

Tyler drops his controller. "Those people need my help."

He activates the device on his wrist. **"GAMER, TRANSFORM!"** he says.

Tyler turns into **the Gamer** and enters the digital realm.

CHAPTER 3

DANGER AT EVERY TURN

The Gamer arrives in the *Space Racers* game.

"**LOOK OUT!**" screams one of the racers.

The Gamer hits the ground as the prisoners blaze past him.

Before the Gamer can get up,
another racer arrives.

This racer's car is **dangerous**.
It is armed with weapons.

In the car sits an evil **monster**.

"Out of my way! I'll **smash** those racers into space dust!" screams the monster. It blazes by.

"Not if I can help it," says the Gamer. "**TurboCraft, activate!**"

The Gamer's special car appears. He hops in.

"Let's go **save** some racers!" he cries.

CHAPTER 4

TO RACE A MONSTER

Driving his TurboCraft, the Gamer races on the track. He passes the monster.

Rockets fire from the monster's car.

The Gamer swerves away from the rockets as they hit a **mountain**.

Chunks of mountain fly toward the racers.

The monster laughs. "Those rocks will be their **doom**."

The Gamer fires all the TurboCraft's lasers.

CHOOM! CHOOM!

The rocks **explode** as the racers continue.

"We're safe," one of the prisoners says.

"Not for long!" the other says, pointing.

The racers are headed toward a **huge compactor**!

"They're going to be smashed to bits if I don't hurry," says the Gamer.

CHAPTER 5

THE FINAL DRIVE

Touching a screen, the Gamer says, **"Activate tractor beam!"**

The tractor beam fires. The beam pulls the trapped racers' cars close to the TurboCraft.

With the racers' cars now close, the Gamer can help. He pulls out his **laser gun**.

He fires a **laser** and **blasts** the car doors open. The trapped racers are free!

"Hop in the TurboCraft. That monster is on our tail!" yells the Gamer.

The monster's car bumps the TurboCraft as they near the compactor.

"I'm going to **destroy** you, Gamer!" the monster roars. It launches more deadly rockets.

"If the rockets don't get you, the **compactor** will!" screams the monster.

"That's what you think!" yells the Gamer. "Let's get out of here."

The deadly rockets are close to the TurboCraft.

But then the TurboCraft shoots out a beam. The beam creates an **opening** to the real world.

The TurboCraft zooms into the opening. The opening quickly closes behind the car.

The opening sends out a burst of energy as it shuts. The blast **destroys** the rockets.

As the rockets explode, the monster loses control of its car. It crashes into the nearby compactor.

In her lair, Cynthia Cyber **roars**. "The next time, the Gamer won't be so lucky!"

GLOSSARY

activate (AK-tuh-vayt)—to turn on or to become active

compactor (kuhm-PAK-ter)—a machine that presses together and crushes objects

digital realm (DIJ-ih-tuhl RELM)—a world created by video games, phone apps, and the internet

prisoner (PRIZ-uh-ner)—a person who is kept against his or her will

ransom (RAN-suhm)—money that must be paid in order to free someone who has been taken prisoner

tractor beam (TRAK-ter BEEM)—a device that attracts and pulls in one object to another from a distance

transform (trans-FORM)—to change one's appearance

TALK ABOUT IT

1. What do you like most about the Gamer? What qualities make him a hero?

2. Discuss the monster racer. What does it look like? Why did Cynthia Cyber create the monster?

WRITE ABOUT IT

1. The book begins with Cynthia Cyber putting her prisoners into a video game. Write a story about how she captured them.

2. What is your favorite illustration in the book? Why? Write a paragraph that argues for your choice.

THE AUTHOR

Shawn Pryor is the creator and co-author of the graphic novel mystery series Cash and Carrie, co-creator and author of the 2019 Glyph-nominated football/drama series Force, and author of *Kentucky Kaiju* and *Diamond Double Play*, from Jake Maddox Sports Stories. In his free time, he enjoys reading, cooking, listening to streaming music playlists, and talking about why Zack from *Mighty Morphin Power Rangers* is the greatest superhero of all time.

THE ILLUSTRATOR

Francesca Ficorilli was born and lives in Rome, Italy. Francesca knew that she wanted to be an artist since she was a child. She was encouraged by her love for animation and her mother's passion for fine arts. After earning a degree in animation, Francesca started working as a freelance animator and illustrator. She finds inspirations for her illustrations in every corner of the world.